The My

and
Mr Midnight

Martin Waddell

Blackie

British Library Cataloguing in Publication Data
Waddell, Martin
The mystery squad and mr midnight.
I. Title
823′ . 914 [J]   PZ7

ISBN 0-216-91421-3
ISBN 0-216-91420-5 Pbk

The Blackie Publishing Group
Bishopbriggs, Glasgow G64 2NZ
Furnival House, 14/18 High Holborn
London WC1V 6BX

Printed in Great Britain by
Thomson Litho Ltd, East Kilbride, Scotland

Are You a Good Detective?

To solve this case you have to follow the trail wherever it leads you and spot the clues on the way. Some are in the story, some are in the pictures. If you crack the clues first time you get maximum points and end up with a Sherlock Holmes Detective Rating. If you don't, you may find further clues to help you but Beware of Custard Pies!

Add up your points as you go along and check your final score against the Detective Rating Chart on page 95. You'll find out how good you really are!

A book for Tom, Simon and Peter

The Mystery begins here . . .

1

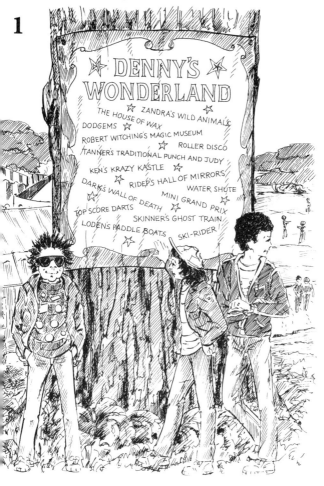

'You look daft in those sunglasses, Bodge,' Beans said.

'No I don't,' I said.

'Don't chew gum while you're talking,' Beans said, so I blew a bubble at her. Actually I wasn't chewing gum. The gum was in my mouth all right, but it was part of my Reversashirt DI (Double Identity) kit.

'You look like a fat ape in that outfit, Bodger,' said Beans. 'A baboon, or something.'

'A Bodger-oon!' said James.

'Ha-ha,' I said.

'Where's Casey got to?' Beans demanded, impatiently. 'No good leaving us code messages to arrange meetings, if he doesn't turn up himself. That's not like Casey.'

'He's gone to the funfair,' I said. 'I bet he's on the dodgems.' They didn't pay any attention to me. 'You're all scared to go on the dodgems with me because I am MSWDC,' I said. I waited for them to ask me what MSWDC meant, but they didn't. 'Mystery Squad World Dodgem Champion!' I said.

'Bodgeroon!'

'At least I'm ready for action,' I said.

'In that outfit?'

The Reversashirt DI kit was James's idea, but I made it myself. It's called a kit because you have to have a comb and bubble gum and specs. The comb is for brushing your hair forward to make it look different. The bubble gum is for sticking on your gums to change the shape of your face. The specs are specs. The Reversashirt is for Mystery Squad members on special operations.

If I get spotted on surveillance, I can change identity in an instant. It's brilliant, whatever Beans says.

This is it.

Here I am (twice) to prove it.

'You haven't even got your notebook with you, you've been so busy with your ape-suit,' said Beans.

'Yes I have,' I said, and I pulled it out of my Secret Pocket.

1

I am not going to tell you where my Secret Pocket is because that is Mystery Squad TSM (Top Secret Material) available on a need-to-know basis only. I am in charge of all Mystery Squad TSM and I decide who needs to know. Casey Peters is the Chief of the Mystery Squad because his dad is a detective and Casey knows about police methods. My brother James is our TE (Technical Expert) and my sister Beans is responsible for code messages when she's not mucking me about.

'I bet you got Casey's message wrong,' I said to Beans. 'It's ten past three, and he hasn't turned up yet.'

'I didn't,' said Beans, and she pulled out the secret message that Casey had left for us at the cafe.

Got the message?

If you can decipher the message turn to section **31**.
If you need help turn to section **29**.

2

Turn to **91** and try again.

3

Turn to **18** and try again.

4

Casey didn't necessarily use sticks and stones to make his sign. Go to **31**.

5

You've gone wrong. Turn to **111** and try again.

6

You've gone wrong. Turn to **48** and try again.

7

You're on the right path. Why? When you know, move to **111**.

8

Right. Where is he? Find him in the big picture in **96**. Then turn to **17**.

9

You're on the right path. Why? When you know, move to **48**.

Detective Rating

5 points if you spotted that the bits of paper fitted together.
Deduct 1 if you needed a clue.
Deduct 1 for each wrong choice.

10   Little Show Man.

'It's MAN,' said James. 'These pieces fit together like a jigsaw puzzle.'

'Eh?'

'Mr Midnight cut the original piece of paper up to get the bits of words he needed for his message. Which doesn't help us very much . . . unless there is something written on the other side of the paper.'

James flipped the three pieces of paper over, and pushed the ends together.

'Nice shiny paper, too,' he murmured. 'Like an advertising thing.'

The S murt T ricks Cat

'The Smart Tricks Cat,' I said. 'What's that, some sort of Pantomime Act?'

'I don't think it's that sort of "Cat" at all,' said James, and he went to get the yellow pages directory.

Complete the Cat

Cat + burglar . . .   Turn to **22**.
Cat + ch . . .   Turn to **60**.
Cat + alogue . . .   Turn to **67**.
Cat + acombs . . .   Turn to **101**.

11

Turn to **18** and try again.

12

Right. Why? Turn to **10**.

13

Turn to **91** and try again.

14

Right. You're about to stumble on Bodger. Turn to **43**.

15

I've already handed it to you on a plate! Turn to **49**.

Detective Rating

3 points for the right answer.
Deduct 1 point for each mistake.

16

'Mr Midnight left a clue on the skull of one of the skeletons,' said James. 'D is the fourth letter of the alphabet and L is the twelfth letter. The sign means four/twelve. But twelve is another way of saying Midnight. This is Mr Midnight's fourth crime.'

'Is it?' said Casey.

'James has gone nuts,' said Beans.

'Agreed,' I said.

'Wait,' said Casey. 'You said there was another of these signs?'

'He'd left a five/twelve sign at the Punch and Judy,' said James. 'He's numbering the places he wrecks!'

'Five/twelve?' said Casey. 'That would be E/L, right? E is the fifth letter of the alphabet, so it must be!'

16

'No,' said James. 'The sign Mr Midnight used for five/twelve at Toby Tanner's is much more difficult to spot.'

Spot the sign!

Look at the picture below.
Is it . . .
sign 1? Turn to **103**.
sign 2? Turn to **94**.
sign 3? Turn to **80**.
sign 4? Turn to **76**.
sign 5? Turn to **56**.

If you need a clue turn to **88**.

Detective Rating

4 points if you spotted the right answer first time.
2 points if it was just a case of mistaken identity.
1 point for the right answer second time round.

17

'There goes Witching,' I said. 'He's creeping off into the bushes near the electric generator with a suitcase.'

'Off you go, Bodge,' said Casey.

'Be careful,' said James. 'Don't on any account go near him, and don't keep on going if you lose him . . . he might have spotted you, and be setting a trap to nab you. So long as you can see him, follow him. If you lose him, stop, and come back.'

'Remember we'll be backing you up,' said Casey. 'Got your notebook?'

I nodded.

'Then you know the tracking signs. We'll be looking out for them.'

Off I went on my Special Undercover Tailing Assignment for the Mystery Squad!

Can you follow my trail?

Look at my notebook. Can you spot the signs I left and work out what they mean? It's the *shape* of the sign that counts.

gone home		this way	
gone home		this way to water	
turn left		this way over obstacle	
turn right		keep going	
not this way		trail divides	
not this way		this way	
this way		not this way	
		this way	
message at 4 paces in direction of arrow			
keep going (trail marker)			

Find the way I went.

Detective Rating

2 points for the right answer straight away.
1 point if you made one mistake.
0 points if you made more than one mistake.

18

'"K.O. Blow",' said Beans. 'What is a K.O. blow?'

'It's a knock-out punch,' I said.

'PUNCH!' said Casey, grinning. 'Punch and Judy!'

'"A little play" and "A one man show",' said James. 'Punch and Judy is a little play, and one man works the puppets.'

'Where's the Punch and Judy stall?' I asked, but nobody knew, so we had to go looking for it. When we found it, there wasn't much left to see.

'What are you lot staring at?' The man who was clearing up the mess stood up. 'No show today. You may as well clear off. Toby Tanner's is closed, and likely to stay closed for good.'

He didn't look friendly, but that was hardly surprising.

'Mr Tanner?' said Casey, putting on his polite voice. Casey is usually very good at getting people to answer questions but it didn't work this time!

'What's it to you, toffee nose?' said Tanner.

'We heard that Mr Midnight had visited your Punch and Judy show, Mr Tanner,' Casey said.

'You heard right, didn't you?' said Tanner. 'Seen enough? I'm busy. I got no time for kids nosing into my affairs.'

'We're not kids, we're the Myster . . . *OUCH!*'
James's foot came down on my toe, hard.

'Clear off!' said Tanner. 'And don't step on anything on the way out!'

We left the Punch and Judy stall.

'Mr Midnight must be really sick to do that,' I said.

'Mad,' said Casey. 'I mean crazy-nutter mad.'

'It could have been done by kids,' said Beans.

'Kids don't leave warning notes beforehand,' said Casey.

'MAD HATTER WRECKS WONDERLAND,'
I said, but nobody laughed.

'At least we know Denny was telling the truth,' said Casey. 'Someone is going round wrecking his funfair.'

'Unless he's doing it himself to claim the insurance money,' said James.

'Funny way to do it, putting his own fair out of business,' Casey said.

James shook his head. 'Denny runs the fair, but the sideshow owners own the sideshows. They pay Denny a proportion of what they take. The more money a show makes, the more money Denny gets.'

'So if Toby Tanner's was a dud show, it would suit Mr Denny to make Toby Tanner give up, so that he could put a more profitable sideshow in its place?'

'Could be,' said James. 'Then again, perhaps Denny *does* own some of the sideshows . . . there's no way we can find that out.'

'So what do we do now?' Beans asked.

'Take another card,' said Casey.

'Another?'

'I've got three of them,' said Casey. 'The K.O. Blow one, and these two.'

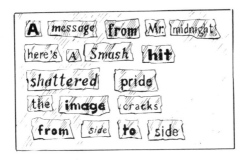

A message from Mr. midnight
here's A Smash hit
shattered pride
the image cracks
from side to side

Beans grabbed the two cards.

'Let somebody else have a look,' I protested.

'Sorry,' she said, 'but I'm the word-game expert round here.'

'Modest, isn't she?' said Casey.

'Nobody can accuse *you* of being modest, Casey,' said James.

'Stop arguing,' said Beans, impatiently. 'We have more important things to attend to. This card, for a start. I think I've worked it out. It's much simpler than the last one. Bonaparte!'

'What?'

'Napoleon's name,' said Beans.

'We know Bonaparte is Napoleon's name,' Casey said, 'but there isn't a sideshow owner called Bonaparte and there certainly isn't any sign of Napoleon.'

'Not Bonaparte,' said Beans. 'Think what it sounds like.'

'It sounds like Bonaparte,' I said, but I couldn't see what she was getting at.

'Or Boney-Part?' she said.

'Eh?'

'Where would you play a "Bloody Game" to get at

the "bony part" of something?' Beans asked. 'Come on, you're all so smart! I know exactly where we should go next.'

Where would you go?

Roller Disco? Turn to **3**.

Dodgems? Turn to **26**.

Tanner's Traditional Punch and Judy? Turn to **92**.

The House of Wax? Turn to **63**.

Robert Witching's Magic Museum? Turn to **104**.

Ken's Krazy Kastle? Turn to **34**.

Zandra's Wild Animals? Turn to **115**.

Ski-Rider? Turn to **107**.

Mini Grand Prix? Turn to **58**.

Top Score Darts? Turn to **120**.

Water Shute? Turn to **45**.

Loden's Paddle Boats? Turn to **72**.

Dark's Wall of Death? Turn to **82**.

Ridep's Hall of Mirrors? Turn to **11**.

Skinner's Ghost Train? Turn to **49**.

NEED A CLUE? Turn to **41**.

19

Turn to **91** and try again.

20

How are jigsaw puzzles made?
Now turn to **42** again.

21

Wrong. Turn to **31**.

22

Wrong. Try again. Turn to **10**.

23

Warning! Cardust Sipe approaching. Turn to **80** and think again.

24

You were warned by the sign. Turn to **111**.

Detective Rating

4 points if you got it right first time.
Deduct 1 point for each mistake.

25

'Nothing here!' I said.

'I knew there wouldn't be,' said Casey.

'You didn't!' said Beans. 'You're just saying that because we didn't find anything.'

'I'm not,' said Casey. 'There wasn't much chance of a clue being here, was there?'

Why not?

If you know turn to **62**.
If you need a clue, turn to **90**.

26

Turn to **18** and try again.

27

Wrong. Turn to **42**.

28

Turn to **91** and try again.

29

Square shows P+ and a picture of Noah's Ark.
"P" plus "ARK" = "PARK".
Go to 1.

30

Now where?

Detective Rating

4 points for the whole message right.
3 points if you needed a clue.
Deduct 1 point for each mistake.
4 or more mistakes, 0 points.

31

'"MEET/AT/TREE/IN/PARK/3 O'CLOCK/CASEY",'
said Beans. 'That's the message. But where is
Casey?'

'It isn't like Casey to let us down,' said James.

Then I did my brilliant bit! A Mystery Squad member has to be observant at all times and I am.

'Casey didn't let us down,' I said and I flipped over the pages of my TSM notebook. 'There!'

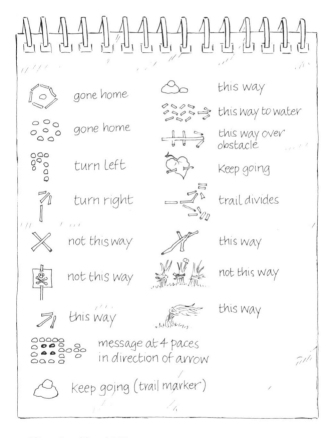

gone home

gone home

turn left

turn right

not this way

not this way

this way

message at 4 paces in direction of arrow

keep going (trail marker)

this way

this way to water

this way over obstacle

keep going

trail divides

this way

not this way

this way

'So what?' said Beans.

'Scout tracking signs,' I said. 'I've been working on them with Casey.'

'Everybody knows about those,' said Beans. 'I did them *ages* ago.'

'You're not so hot at spotting them, are you?' I said.

'What do you mean, Bodge?' said James.

'I mean that Casey has been here, and he's left a message for us. He's also left a sign telling us where to look for it.'

Spot the Sign?

Sign 1 . . . turn to **100**.
Sign 2 . . . turn to **21**.
Sign 3 . . . turn to **53**.
Sign 4 . . . turn to **91**.
Sign 5 . . . turn to **74**.
Need a clue? Turn to **4**.

32

Wrong. Turn to **42**.

33

Turn to **91** and try again.

34

Turn to **18** and try again.

35

Wrong. Look at the picture in **96** and try again.

36

Wrong. Turn to **112** and try again.

37

You've gone wrong. Turn to **17** and try again.

38

You've gone wrong. Turn to **111** and try again.

39

Wrong. Turn to **43**.

40

You've gone wrong. Turn to **48** and try again.

41

It keeps your outside out and your inside in. Need another clue? Turn to **15**. If you don't, turn to **49**.

Detective Rating

3 points if you got it first time.
2 points if you made one mistake.

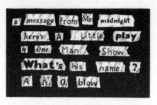

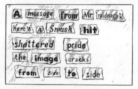

42

James took out his tweezers.

'What are you doing?' Casey asked.

'Just a little experiment,' James said.

And the next moment, before anyone could stop him, he had peeled off the word LITTLE from the card.

Casey went pale. 'That's *evidence*! You can't interfere with evidence.'

James looked grim. 'It's worth it, if it means we can stop this blackmailer,' he said.

'But you're ripping the card up!'

'I'm not,' James said. 'I'm just peeling off one or two of the words!' As he said it, he succeeded in peeling the word SHOW off the card. Then he scraped the glue off the back.

'But . . .'

'I'm picking out words that belong together, in the hope that I may get a fresh lead on Mr Midnight,' explained James. 'It so happens there are three of them on this card.'

What is the third word?

Message . . . Turn to **64**.

From . . .Turn to **27**.

Mr . . . Turn to **98**.

Midnight . . . Turn to **32**.

Here's . . . Turn to **46**.

Play . . . Turn to **84**.

One . . . Turn to **106**.

Man . . . Turn to **12**.

What's . . . Turn to **59**.

Name . . . Turn to **114**.

Anything else? Turn to **123**.

Need a clue? Turn to **20**.

Detective Rating

3 points for every path you got right first time.
1 point for every path you got right second time round.

43

Witching had stopped, so I stopped too.

He was in the middle of a clearing. I crouched in the bushes, waiting for something to happen. I was hoping the others had seen my signs. I had used

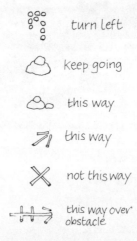

	turn left
	keep going
	this way
	this way
	not this way
	this way over obstacle

Then I had a terrifying idea. Perhaps he was going to set fire to the trees, and I would be trapped. But then, so would he.

'Bodge?' Casey whispered. They had crept up without me hearing them.

'What's he up to, Bodge?' Casey said.

'Watch!' I said.

'Money!' Beans said. 'But if he is Mr Midnight, what is he doing leaving money here?'

'Don't you see?' said Casey. 'We were wrong. Witching *isn't* Mr Midnight. He can't be!'

'Witching *isn't* Mr Midnight?'

'It's obvious that Witching is *being blackmailed.*

Mr Midnight had threatened to wreck his collection. Mr Midnight proved he could do it by destroying the other sideshows. This was supposed to be the pay-off.'

'But . . .'

'Witching is nuts about his collection. You remember the fuss he made when he thought we'd damaged it? He would pay anything rather than run the risk of his precious collection being damaged.'

'What do we do now?' said James. 'Stay and spot the blackmailer when he comes to collect?'

'Oh no we *don't*,' said Casey, firmly. 'We can't tackle criminals on our own. My dad would put an absolute stop on the Squad if we tried it. What we do now is to go as fast as we can for help. Dad will stake the place out with half a dozen large policemen and they can do the fighting.'

'I bet we could tackle Mr Midnight,' I said. 'We could jump him from behind and . . .'

'NO!' said Casey firmly.

'He's right, Bodge,' said James.

'But . . .'

'No buts about it,' said Casey. 'Mr Midnight is a violent criminal, and that is all there is to it. We can't tackle him ourselves.'

'Agreed!' said James.

'In which case, we have no time to muck about,' said Beans. 'Let's get weaving!'

We went back the way we'd come, to fetch Casey's dad and get him to set up a trap to catch Mr Midnight, when he came to collect the blackmail money Witching had left in the wood.

We didn't find Casey's dad, but Casey spotted one of the plainclothes men and told him.

The plainclothes man started to laugh and then he talked to Casey for a long time, explaining something.

Casey went green!

'What's the matter, Casey?' James said, when the plainclothes man had gone.

'It's Robert Witching,' said Casey. 'He's been arrested!'

'*Arrested?*'

Casey nodded. 'Witching *is* Mr Midnight.'

'But he can't be. That would mean he was black-mailing *himself*!'

'He *must* be,' said Casey. 'Apparently he was caught in the act by Mr Skinner, trying to burn down the Krazy Kastle. Witching made a run for it, not knowing whether Skinner had seen enough to identify him . . .'

'But we've been with Witching from the time we saw him with his suitcase up until a few minutes ago!' I said.

'Skinner's absolutely positive it was Witching he saw,' said Casey.

'We must have seen Witching *after* he'd run away from Skinner,' said James. 'I mean, he couldn't know whether Skinner had made a positive identi-fication or not, could he?'

Casey shrugged. 'Suppose not,' he said.

'Well then. He had two choices. He could run, in which case he was as good as admitting that he *was* Mr Midnight, or he could stay and bluff it out. The business with the suitcase and the money and the note addressed to Mr Midnight is Witching's attempt to cover his tracks.'

'You mean he did it so that he could say he was in

the woods when the Krazy Kastle business happened, waiting for Mr Midnight?' said Casey.

'Exactly,' said James. 'I bet our friend Witching is in there now, busily denying that he was ever near the Krazy Kastle, and trying to bluff everybody into believing that he was being blackmailed.'

'The police are searching for the suitcase . . .' said Casey.

'We were right after all,' said Beans. 'Witching is Mr Midnight! I always thought he was.'

'How did Skinner manage to catch him at it?' I asked.

'Witching was too clever by half. He delivered two more of his advance warning notes . . . but this time Skinner managed to figure out where Mr Midnight was going to strike next . . . the Krazy Kastle.'

'He's caught now,' said Beans.

'Is he?' said James. 'It will be his word against Skinner's!'

'No it *won't*,' said Beans. 'We can tell your dad about the catalogue with the message words cut out of it , Casey. It's in Witching's office.'

'He'll say it was planted there . . .'

'So what?' said Beans. 'I always thought Mr Midnight was Witching. The whole Mr Midnight business is full of tricks . . . the sort of things a magician might try . . .'

Casey looked doubtful.

'Unless Mr Skinner is able to convince a jury about the identification, Witching will probably get away with it,' said James.

Then we saw Skinner. He was standing with Mr Denny, talking to some reporters.

We went across to them.

Skinner was showing off the last two messages, which he had scribbled down on a bit of paper:

> *Summing up*
> *Lives of Fame*
> *As Candles Flicker,*
> *All's aflame!*

'That was the House of Wax,' Skinner said. 'But unfortunately we didn't work it out in time.'

'Got the second rhyme, sir?' asked a reporter.

'Yes.'

> *I strike my light*
> *Within the walls*
> *Of Tom o' Bedlam's*
> *Hallowed Halls.*

'Tom o' Bedlam,' said Skinner. 'That's what they used to call lunatics. So I worked out that Tom o' Bedlam's Hallowed Halls meant the Krazy Kastle!'

'I'd have got that, if I'd seen it,' muttered Beans.

Casey's dad appeared. He didn't look pleased when he saw what Skinner was up to. He headed straight for the little group.

'Everyone was watching the firemen fight the fire,' said Skinner. 'I reckon Mr Midnight thought no-one would be paying attention to what was happening at the other side of the fair . . . and no-one was, but me!'

'That will do for now, gentlemen,' said Casey's dad, pushing through the crowd.

'Oh, come on, Inspector Peters!' one of the reporters objected. 'We've got to get our story.'

'You can say that acting upon Mr Skinner's positive identification a man is being questioned by the police, and may be charged with malicious damage to property . . .'

'Let him finish his story, Boss!' said another reporter, an older man. 'Go on, Mr Skinner.'

'There isn't much to say,' said Skinner. 'I went down to the Krazy Kastle and there he was, large as life, with petrol sprinkled round the place, and matches. It was W . . .'

'That's enough, Mr Skinner,' said Casey's dad, in a warning voice.

'It was Robert Witching,' Skinner blurted out. 'Robert Witching is Mr Midnight . . . I saw him.'

Suddenly Casey was moving. He pushed through the crowd, and grabbed his dad by the arm.

'Skinner's lying, Dad,' he said.

'Casey,' snapped his dad, 'I've had enough trouble with you and your . . .'

'Dad! Listen! Mr Skinner's lying. His story hinges on the fact that Robert Witching used the excitement of the firemen fighting the fire as cover when he went to the Krazy Kastle.'

'So what?' said Skinner.

Can you prove Skinner was lying?

Turn to the big picture in **96**.
Is it to do with the position of . . .
Robert Witching, the dodgems and the House of Wax? Turn to **39**.
Robert Witching, the men with buckets, and the direction of the wind? Turn to **110**.
Robert Witching, the fire-engine and the ice cream van? Turn to **119**.

44

Turn to **91** and try again.

45

Turn to **18** and try again.

46

Wrong. Turn to **42**.

47

Right. How did she do it?
If you need a clue turn to **116**.
If you know how she did it turn to **81**.

48

Now where?

Detective Rating

6 points if you got it right without help.
5 points if you consulted the clue section first.
Deduct 1 point for each mistake you made.
More than 5 mistakes, 0 points.
0 points if you were custard-pied!

49

'The Ghost Train,' said Beans. 'Skinners!'

I gaped at her.

'You skin something, that's playing a "bloody game" to get at the "bony-part"—that's Napoleon's name.'

'Eugh!' I said. 'What sort of mind would think of that?'

'Mr Midnight's,' said James.

Skinner's Ghost Train had been wrecked, just as we'd expected.

'That's Mr Denny who owns Wonderland,' said Casey. 'The man with the cigar. He's been receiving the notes from Mr Midnight, but he didn't realise what they were until after Mr Midnight had done his wrecking. The other one must be Skinner.'

'Don't like the look of them,' I said.

'Don't judge by appearances,' said James.

Casey went forward into the Ghost Train tunnel, past the wrecked carriages.

'Sorry kid,' said Skinner, turning towards him. 'We're closed.'

Denny looked round. 'Here, don't I know you?' he said.

'We met at the police station, Mr Denny,' Casey said, doing his polite act.

'Nicking bikes, son?' asked Skinner, with a laugh.

'My dad is Detective-Inspector Peters,' said Casey. 'I called in to see him.'

Skinner stopped laughing, double quick!

'Hasn't done much about this lot, has he?' said Denny. 'You tell your dad sending a copper down here to inspect the damage isn't what I need.'

'Don't know what we've got a police force for,' said Skinner.

'I'm sure Dad knows what he's doing,' said Casey, going red.

'Are you?' said Denny. 'I wish I was.'

He turned on his heel and stalked away, almost tripping over the rope as he did so.

'What happened, sir?' asked Casey.

Skinner shrugged. 'Mr Midnight got in here, after the show shut down for the night. You can see what he did yourself.'

'Money taken?' said Casey.

Skinner shook his head.

'Means of entry?' said Casey. He made it sound casual, but he was pumping Skinner for every bit of information he could.

'How should I know?' said Skinner. 'The tunnel doors are closed each night. Who cares how he got in? He did . . . and the result is thousands of pounds worth of damage!'

'As much as that?' said Casey.

'That's the train alone . . . The ghosts are another problem!'

'Seen anybody odd, any prowlers?' James asked.

'I see people all day,' said Skinner. 'This is a funfair, you know.'

'Anybody else got any useful questions?' Casey said, turning to us.

'What is this?' said Skinner. 'The Third Degree?' His face tightened up. 'You leave your questions to your father,' he said to Casey. 'Not everybody likes kids shoving their noses in.'

He turned away, and walked out of the tunnel.

'You blew that, Casey,' said James.

Casey ignored him. 'Anybody got any ideas?'.

'Mr Midnight had duplicate keys,' I said. 'He came round after the place was closed.'

'Which means he's someone who could move around the fairground freely, without being noticed,' said James. 'It would be impossible for an outsider.'

'So we're probably looking for someone who works at Wonderland,' said Casey. 'One of the showmen maybe, or one of the men who look after the machines . . .'

'Suppose Mr Midnight hid inside here, before the Wonderland closed,' said Beans. 'He might not have had a key at all.'

'He could have hidden in the tunnel among the ghosts and things,' said James.

'Bit chancey,' said Casey.

'There's a trapdoor in the ceiling,' I pointed out. 'Mr Midnight could have hung in the roof space, like a demon bat.'

'Bodge,' moaned Beans.

James was wandering round. He stopped in front of the dancing skeletons.

'Midnight,' he said. 'The twelfth hour.'

'So?'

'So . . . he's numbering them!' said James, his face breaking into a grin. 'This is the second one of these I've seen. Five, four, three, two, one . . . he's numbering them!'

'What?' Casey said.

'This is number four,' said James. 'D is the fourth letter of the alphabet.'

'So what?' I said.

'D.L,' said James.

'What does L mean?' I said.

What does L mean?

L stands for mirrors? Turn to **89**.
L stands for museum? Turn to **117**.
L stands for midnight? Turn to **16**.
L stands for magic? Turn to **109**.

50

You're on the right path. Why? When you know, move to **30**.

51

Wrong! Go to **81** and try again.

52

You've gone wrong! Turn to **30** and try again.

53

Wrong. Turn to **31**.

54

Wrong. Turn to **112** and try again.

55

More tricks? Check the last picture in **67**.

56

Wrong. Turn to **16**.

57
Turn to **91** and try again.

58
Turn to **18** and try again.

59
Wrong. Turn to **42**.

60
Wrong. Try again. Turn to **10**.

61

Receive a sweet smelling custard pie and go to **105**.

Detective Rating

2 points if you realised that there had been a clean up.
1 point if you needed a clue to work it out.

62

'The place has been thoroughly cleaned up,' said Casey. 'If there was a clue, it's probably been cleaned up too!'

'There might be something written on the glass fragments,' I said, hopefully.

There was a silence. We all looked at the broken glass.

'We could cut ourselves to pieces looking for it,' said Beans.

'The Brilliant Bodgeroon strikes again,' said James. 'We'd all go home dripping blood.'

'Right,' said Casey. 'On this one we can't prove anything about the countdown signs . . .'

James started to protest.

'Hold on!' said Casey. 'I was trying to say that we ought to think about what the countdown *means*, supposing that the signs aren't just coincidence.'

'It's a countdown,' I said, puzzled, because we had already worked it out. 'Five was Tanners, Four was the Arcade, Three was probably this one. Then Two, One . . .'

'And?'

'BLAST OFF!' I said. 'BOOM-VAROOM!'

Beans gave a yowl.

'That was Beans's nose you hit, Bodger,' said James.

'I didn't mean to,' I said. 'I was only Boom-varooming. Anyway, I've probably improved it.'

'Just be more careful where you swing your arms next time,' said Beans.

I blew a bubble at her. My gum was getting a bit stringy, but I needed it for my disguise.

'If the countdown signs are being left by Mr Midnight, they are the opposite of everything else he does. Right?' said Casey.

'Wrong,' said Beans. 'They're just another example of his nuttiness!'

'To make us all *think* he's nuts,' I said.

Casey shook his head. 'Mr Midnight is a show-off. He adopts a fancy nickname, he makes up rhymes telling where he is going to strike next. All to draw attention to his nuttiness. But the countdown signs are different. He *hides* them. It is as if he *didn't* want them to be spotted.'

'Why leave them at all?' said James, and then he blinked. 'Oh! Yes! I see. Well done, Casey!'

They were doing their We-Are-Brilliant-Detectives Double Act. Beans and I were meant to jump about asking them what they had detected.

We waited patiently.

'The countdown signs aren't meant for just any-one,' said Casey. 'They're meant for one particular person . . . somebody who is already on the look out for them.'

'Right!' said James. 'Once I knew what to look for, I spotted them quickly enough.'

'So what?' I said. I didn't think much of their brilliant bit so far.

'Blackmail!' said Casey.

'Uh?' Beans gave up inspecting her boom-varoomed nose.

'The person being blackmailed knows what's meant to happen when the countdown finishes,' said Casey.

'Blast off time!' I said.

'Right,' said Casey. 'It makes sense of the other crimes, the meaningless-looking ones. Mr Midnight is showing someone that he means business. He's threatening to do something big . . . and demonstrating that he can do it by wrecking these other places.'

'So the *important* crime hasn't happened yet?' Beans said.

'Exactly. Blast off is getting closer and closer, and if whoever's being blackmailed doesn't pay up . . .'

We all thought about it.

'We'll have to warn Dad that this isn't a case of somebody vandalising a funfair for kicks,' said Casey.

We went to see Casey's dad.

'We think it's blackmail, Dad,' said Casey.

'Evidence?' said Casey's dad.

'The only hard evidence we have is the warning notes,' Casey said. 'The rest is just deduction.'

'You mean the notes that Mr Denny showed me this morning?' asked Casey's dad.

Casey nodded.

'I wasn't impressed then, and I'm not impressed now.'

Casey told him our theory, all over again.

'I'll need more evidence than this before I can send the number of men I would need to cover the funfair on a twenty-four hour basis,' said Casey's dad. 'I'm not saying you're wrong, but your theory is just a theory.

I have much more important things on my mind than an outbreak of glass-breaking at a funfair.'

'But if somebody is being blackmailed, Dad . . .'

'Blackmail is a very serious crime, and I would be interested. Very interested. That's a different story. But as it is I have a pile of work here this evening and I don't want to hear another word about it from you lot. Okay?'

'Okay, Dad,' said Casey reluctantly.

'Listen, Casey. Here's some cash. Take your friends to the cinema, eh? It'll do you more good than hanging around a place like that.'

'Not tonight, thanks Dad,' said Casey.

He didn't take the money.

We all went out to Casey's garage, to have an MSM.

'You should have taken the money, Casey,' I said. 'We could all have gone to the pictures.'

'Shut up, Bodge,' said James. 'What's your dad up to, Casey?' he asked.

'He's not keen on us hanging around the funfair and he certainly is working on the case!' said Casey. 'He wants to keep us out of trouble, I suppose.'

'He said he *wasn't* working on the case,' Beans objected.

'He didn't,' said Casey. 'He said he didn't want to hear another word from us about it. That doesn't mean *he's* not working on it.'

'We have clear evidence that he is working on it, *now*,' said James.

What clear evidence?

If you know, turn to **105**.
If you need a clue turn to **70**.

63

Turn to **18** and try again.

64

Wrong. Turn to **42**.

65

Turn to **91** and try again.

66

Compare this picture with the first picture in **67**.

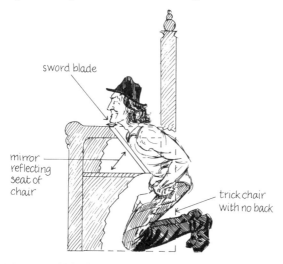

sword blade

mirror reflecting seat of chair

trick chair with no back

The sword blade conceals the top edge of the mirror, which is placed to reflect the seat of the chair as though it were the back of the chair. Robert Witching can kneel behind the mirror and his body is hidden from view.

Now turn to **96**.

Detective Rating

3 points if you knew it was a catalogue.
Deduct 1 point for each wrong answer.

67

The S mart T ricks Cat

'Smart Tricks Limited, 15 Union Street,' said James, closing the telephone directory. 'I was right. Smart Tricks Ltd. is a joke shop, and the Cat is their Catalogue.'

'Brilliant,' said Beans.

'Not bad, James,' said Casey.

'So Mr Midnight is someone who uses tricks and magical equipment,' said James. 'The sort of person who might have a Smart Tricks Catalogue hanging about the place.'

'There's a Magic Museum in Wonderland,' I said.

'Robert Witching's Magic Museum,' said Casey.

'Which makes R. Witching *R* Number One Suspect!' said Beans. 'Get it? R is Our suspect!' She thinks she's very funny.

Which is how we came to be back in Wonderland, at the entrance to Robert Witching's Magic Museum, half an hour later.

'How do you feel about being a burglar, Casey?' said James, grimly. 'Think your dad will be pleased?'

'We're not going to take anything,' Casey said. 'We're just going to look.'

'What *for*?'

'Anything . . . anything at all that might confirm what we suspect: that Robert Witching is Mr Midnight.'

'Like a Smart Tricks Catalogue with bits cut out,' I suggested.

'Right,' said Casey.

We went inside the Magic Museum, and trailed around behind the crowd for the first few minutes. It was a weird place, like a dark maze, with Witching's magical effects suddenly lighting it up.

'Look at that!' gasped Beans.

'That's him!' said Casey, in my ear. 'Witching himself.'

'But . . .' The trouble was I could see Witching's head, but I couldn't see Witching.

His head started to tell us about his Museum.

'Come on, Bodge,' Casey said.

I slipped away after the others into the darkness.

'I hope we don't meet the rest of Robert Witching, wandering round,' Beans said.

'It's a trick,' Casey said.

'All done with mirrors, probably,' said James.

'Yes, but HOW?'

'Shut up, Bodge,' said James and Casey together.

There were lots of little rooms and the place was spooky, because when you walked into a new room, the light went on, and things flashed at you. The first time it happened we almost had heart attacks, but then we got used to it.

'Search!' said Casey, and we went on down the corridor, away from the sound of the crowd.

We were in the room with Houdini's Escape Gear when I made my mistake. There was a Coke tin, and I said 'I bet Houdini didn't drink Coke' and picked it up.

'OUCH!'

I got an electric shock, right up my arm. It was another one of Robert Witching's spooky jokes like the lights that went on and off. It was meant as a joke, but my yell made it serious.

'Quick!' James said. 'There's someone coming.'

My shout had given us away.

We nipped out of that room and into the next one.

The light flashed on, which was just what we didn't want it to do . . . and it showed we were in a trap. There was no way out, except the way we had come *in*. The room was like a little theatre, with seats and a stage.

'Up on to the stage!' said Casey. 'There may be a stage door, behind the curtains.'

It was a big mistake!

We had fallen into something. As we lay there, the light went out.

Then another light went on, blazing right into our faces.

We were in a pit below the stage but we were up above us too.

The main lights went on, and we disappeared from the stage above us, at the same time as Witching appeared, glaring down at us.

'Out!' he said.

'Pepper's Ghost!' said James.

'Oh! So that's it!' said Witching. 'Amateur Magicians, trying to steal some of my tricks. We'll see about that . . .'

'I wasn't trying to steal your tricks,' said James. 'I read about that one in . . .'

'You're coming to my office!' Witching growled. His face was red with anger! 'Sit there,' he said, when he'd got us to the office. 'And don't move!'

He stormed out of the room.

'H-E-L-P,' said Beans, weakly.

'Why didn't you shut up about Pepper's Ghost?' said Casey. 'It really made him mad, that did.'

'What is it?' I said.

'Pepper's Ghost? It's the name of a trick,' said James. 'That one. We were Pepper's Ghosts, for a minute.'

'And now Witching thinks we are amateur magicians, trying to sneak round and pinch his tricks,' said Casey. 'What a mess!'

Robert Witching came storming back into the office, with . . . Casey's dad.

'Oh, no! More trouble from you blessed kids!'

Casey's dad looked mad!

'Smashing up my equipment, trying to steal professional secrets,' said Robert Witching, almost doing a dance. 'I've had enough. I want these children charged ·. .'

'I . . .er . . . know these children,' said Casey's dad. 'One of them is my . . . er . . . son.' If looks could have killed, Casey would have been dead and buried on the spot.

'Your son! Your SON! My equipment is priceless. It cannot be replaced. If anything has been damaged . . .'

'I assure you that any damage will be paid for,' said Casey's dad, grimly.

Witching went on, and on and on, as if we'd stolen the crown jewels. We couldn't get a word in edgewise. And when he'd finished, Casey's dad started in.

Then Mr Denny turned up and the whole thing had to be explained again.

'They think of themselves as detectives,' said Casey's dad.

'And their way of detecting is to creep around causing trouble is it, Inspector?' said Denny, icily.

'I expect the police when I call the police, not a pack of children!'

'You've got the police, Mr Denny,' said Casey's dad. 'You've had them all day, as I've already explained to you.'

'I haven't seen them, then!' said Denny.

'Plain clothes men, Mr Denny,' said Casey's dad. 'I don't think uniformed policemen would have been much help in this situation, do you?'

'And I suppose these children are a plain clothes detail as well?' said Denny icily.

'These children were acting entirely on their own initiative,' said Casey's dad. 'They'll have me to answer to.'

'I demand that these children be dealt with!' said Robert Witching.

'I'm sure Inspector Peters will manage to cope with these tiny criminals, Robert, even if he can't catch the fully grown variety,' said Denny icily. 'Check if they've done any damage, will you? I have Skinner round my neck claiming a small fortune for destruction at his place, not to mention Toby and Mr Ridep.'

Witching went off trying to find if we'd bust any of his fancy exhibits, and we spent some uncomfortable minutes with Casey's dad. He did all the talking.

'You didn't tell him what we've found out,' Beans complained, when we finally escaped.

'He was in no mood to be told about anything,' said Casey, gloomily.

'It was worth a telling off,' said James. 'At least we know we're working on the right lines in suspecting Witching.'

'Do we?' said Beans.

Casey looked at James, and laughed.

'You're hopeless, Beans,' I said. 'Can't spot the evidence, even when it's right under your nose!

What evidence?

You know . . . Turn to **96**.
You need a clue? Turn to **55**.

*If you want to know how Robert Witching's talking head illusion worked, turn to **66**.*

*If you want to know how the Pepper's Ghost trick worked, turn to **69**.*

Detective Rating

*If you spotted straight away that Witching had left before
the firemen arrived take 5 points.*
Deduct 1 point for each wrong choice.

68

'We followed Witching into the wood before the
firemen got here, Dad,' said Casey. 'I know it was
before they started fighting the fire, because there
was a rumpus at the gates. Someone had parked an
ice cream van there. The firemen had to move the ice
cream van to get their fire engine in.'

Skinner went pale.

'Nonsense!' he blustered. 'You're muddled up.
You got it wrong!'

'I've got three witnesses,' said Casey.

'Us!' we all said.

'Well, Mr Skinner,' said Casey's dad. 'It looks as if you have some explaining to do, doesn't it?'

But Skinner had no intention of staying to explain anything . . . he would have been clean away, but Casey's dad was too quick for him.

Skinner was copped!

It didn't take long for Casey's dad to get the full story out of him. He told us all about it over our Celebration Chips in the cafe.

'Skinner was losing money on his Ghost Train. He planned to wreck it, claim the compensation money, and try to set up a new show on the proceeds . . . by taking over Robert Witching's very successful Magic Museum. To do that, he had to get rid of Witching. Skinner dreamed up Mr Midnight . . .'

'Don't see why?' said Beans.

'The idea was to frame Witching, by making it seem that he was Mr Midnight.'

'Witching is a magician. He's used to tricks and sleight of hand,' James said. 'Just the kind of person Mr Midnight seemed to be.'

'After all, we suspected Witching first,' said Casey. 'He is a bit of a nutcase, after all. Nuts about his collection . . .'

'Exactly,' said Casey's dad. 'Skinner played on that fear. He had Witching convinced that Mr Midnight was out to destroy the Magic Museum, unless Witching paid up. The countdown signs were part of that. Skinner knew that Witching wouldn't go to the police, with his precious collection at risk. Then Witching was sent off into the woods . . . and Skinner sprang his trap.'

'Making sure that Witching had no alibi!' said Casey.

'Yes. With the Smart Tricks Catalogue found in Witching's office, and the evidence of identification, Witching would either have been convicted of the crimes or, at least, forced out of business.'

'Forced out of business?' said Beans.

'Yes,' said Casey's dad. 'Robert Witching is a Showman. Showbusiness is a small world. Would you be prepared to let somebody with a reputation as Mr Midnight set up his show in your fair?'

'Nope!'

'Exactly. Witching would have been in prison or out of business, either way he would have been forced to sell off his collection dirt cheap. Guess who would have been in the market to buy?'

'Skinner!' said Beans.

'But for you kids, it would have worked!' said Casey's dad. 'You did a great job. What about more chips, all round?'

'Good idea!' I said.

'Tell you what,' said Casey's dad. 'Young Bodger, you should offer your whatsit . . .'

'Reversashirt Double Identity kit,' I said proudly.

'You should offer it to Robert Witching for his Museum. It is tricky enough.'

'Hold on,' said Beans. 'Do you think Robert Witching would put Bodge in his Museum, as well as his kit?'

'The only Bodgeroon in captivity!' said James.

'Like King Kong!' said Beans.

'Any more chips?' I said, and I waited to see how long it would take Beans to discover she'd been sitting on my chewing gum.

Now look at the Detective Rating Chart on p. 95 to find out how good a Detective you are!

69

Look at the picture below to see how the famous Pepper's Ghost illusion works.

On stage is a mirror which reflects what's happening in the pit. The audience see the reflection.

Now turn to **96**.

70

Got it? Move on to **105**.

71
You've gone wrong. Turn to **111** and try again.

72
Turn to **18** and try again.

73
Turn to **91** and try again.

74
Wrong. Turn to **31**.

75
You've gone wrong. Turn to **17** and try again.

76
Wrong. Turn to **16**.

77
You've gone wrong. Turn to **48** and try again.

78
Wrong. Turn to **105**.

79
Wrong. It's a matter of identity. Turn to **96** and try again.

Detective Rating

4 points if you got it straight away.
3 points if you needed a clue.
Deduct 1 point for each mistake.

80

'The Punch figure was laid out very carefully, with a circle drawn round it. That was what caught my attention. Why should Mr Midnight stop in the middle of wrecking the Punch and Judy to scrape a circle in the sand? Then I noticed the arms of the figure. They looked like the hands of a clock. Five to twelve. I didn't pay much attention to it then, but after I'd spotted D/L and worked out that it could stand for four to twelve, I began to think.'

'*Five*, *four*, three-two-one . . . it's a countdown!' I said.

'A countdown to *what*?' said Casey.

None of us could work it out.

'Mr Midnight is an evil mastermind out to conquer the world,' I said. 'Only the Mystery Squad stand between him and . . .'

'Shut up, Bodge,' said James.

'It is like that, though, isn't it?' said Casey, thoughtfully. 'You'd expect Superman to come swooping down! Someone using a name like Mr Midnight, going around leaving rhyming notes and sprinkling clues that people either won't notice, or won't understand—it seems phoney to me!'

'Mr Midnight belongs in a comic,' said Beans.

'If he isn't a nutcase, we have to explain why someone who is *sane* is doing all these *insane* things,' James said.

'To make people *think* he is insane,' I said.

Casey looked at James. 'That's right,' he said. 'Bodge has worked it out!'

'Well done, Bodge,' said Casey. 'All these nutty things are being done to make everyone *believe* that Mr Midnight is a nutcase.'

'But there *must* be one thing that he really wants to do,' said James. 'He's doing the other things to distract attention from it.'

'So "Mr Midnight" wants to bust up one of the sideshows or commit some other crime, for reasons of his own, and disguise it as being the work of a nutter who goes around busting everything he can lay his hands on?' Casey said.

'Mr Denny could be doing it to get rid of shows that aren't bringing in enough cash,' Beans said.

'Or one of the sideshow men, Skinner or Toby Tanner or somebody else, could be doing it to get rid of his own business and claim compensation money from his insurers,' said James.

'What *for*?' said Beans.

'I don't know,' said James. 'Maybe he wants a holiday in the Bahamas.'

'It's more likely that one of the showmen wants to get rid of a show that's failing, and use the money to buy a new one,' said Casey.

'In other words,' said Beans, 'we are all hopelessly muddled up, and haven't got a clue what's going on.'

James and Casey opened their mouths to protest and then closed them again.

'She's right,' said James.

'I thought I was,' said Beans. 'What do we do now? Go home and give up?'

The Mystery Squad has never yet given up on an investigation.

We all looked at Casey. Casey is Chief of the Mystery Squad. He always knows what to do next.

'Well . . . er . . .' Casey said.

Even Casey was stumped.

'The third card!' I said. Sometimes I think I should be Chief really. I get all the best ideas.

'That's what I was going to say,' said Casey. 'Why don't we . . . er . . see if we can figure out the message on the third card?' He read aloud:

> 'Here's a smash hit
> Shattered pride
> The image cracks
> From side to side.'

'Give it to Beans,' said James. 'She's the one with the crossword puzzle mind.'

'Monkey puzzle,' I said.

Beans was concentrating on the message.

'Well,' said James.

'Shattered pride,' said Beans.

'What about it?'

'You said I had a crossword puzzle mind. Well, if I came across "shattered pride" in a crossword puzzle I know what I would start looking for.'

'An anagram!' said James, and he tried to grab the card back, but Beans wouldn't let him.

'What's an anagram?' I said.

'It's when you muddle up the letters in a word to make it look like another one. Like . . . like . . . P-E-S-T-E-R!' said Beans.

'Thanks a lot!' said Casey.

'I don't get it,' I said.

'P-e-s-t-e-r equals P-e-t-e-r-s,' explained Casey. 'It's one of Beans's little jokes.'

'I'm lost,' I said.

'You usually are,' said Beans. 'Why don't you take off those silly sunglasses and find yourself?'

'What Beans means, Bodge,' said James, 'is that if she came across a clue in a crossword puzzle that said "Pester broken up" it could mean P-e-t-e-r-s, because P-e-s-t-e-r is made up from the same letters as P-e-t-e-r-s.'

'What is Casey's name doing in a crossword puzzle?' I wanted to know, but nobody told me.

'This time,' said James, 'the clue is "shattered pride", which could mean that the letters making up p-r-i-d-e should be arranged another way to help us solve Mr Midnight's message.'

'Sounds stupid to me!' grunted Casey.

Who's right?

Need a clue? Turn to **23**.
James? Turn to **112**.
Casey? Turn to **118**.

Detective Rating

2 points if you solved this straight away.
1 point if you needed a clue.
0 points for anything else.

81

'Beans took the card by slipping her hat over it, when it was lying on the kitchen table,' I said.

But which of the three cards was it?

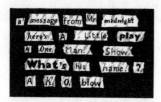

. . . Turn to **42**.

. . . Turn to **51**.

. . . Turn to **99**.

Need to look back . . . Turn to **125**.

82

Turn to **18** and try again.

83

Turn to **91** and try again.

84

Wrong. Turn to **42**.

85

Wrong. Look at the picture in **96** and try again.

86

You've gone wrong. Turn to **17** and try again.

87

Wrong. Turn to **105**.

88

You're looking for a clockface that isn't a clockface. Turn to **16**.

89

Wrong! Turn to **49**.

90

Move on to **62**.

Detective Rating

4 points if you got here straight away.
Deduct 1 if you needed a clue.
Deduct 1 for each mistake you made.
4 or more mistakes, 0 points.

91

'Casey arranged the flowers that were waiting to be bedded out to show "Message hidden at four paces in direction of arrow",' I said. 'He used the last plant to mark the burying place.'

'What does the message say?' said Beans.

Casey's message was rolled up inside a cardboard tube, with sellotape stuck over the ends, to keep damp from getting at it. The sellotape had his initials half on it and half on the side of the tube, so that we would be able to see a break in the initials if it had been disturbed. Casey is very careful about things like that.

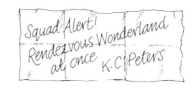

'Rendezvous Wonderland?' said James. 'The Funfair? What for?'

'Maybe we'll all get a ride on the dodgems,' I said.

'You go mad on dodgems,' said Beans, scornfully. 'I'm not going near them if you go on. You whizz around making *buzz* and *zuzz* noises and crashing into people instead of avoiding them. That's not the proper way to drive dodgems.'

I blew a bubble at her.

'Don't waste your bubble gum,' said Beans. 'It is supposed to be part of your disguise. Pity you didn't give him a paper bag to put over his head instead, James,' she added.

'Pudding face,' I said to Beans.

'I think Casey's testing us,' said James, looking round him at the sideshows. 'He's leaving a trail behind him. First the code, then the buried message, and now we're supposed to hunt round the Funfair for him.'

'I don't think he'd have used "Alert" in his message if he was just testing us,' Beans pointed out.

'Where is he then?'

'Right behind you!'

Beans jumped a mile, as Casey's voice sounded in her ear.

We all whirled round.

Casey was grinning at us.

'You weren't very careful, were you?' he said. 'I was at the ice cream van that's parked across the main entrance gates. You went past, didn't spot me, and I trailed you. Not one of you looked round or sensed that you were being followed.'

'So what?' said James, crossly.

'So next time it might matter,' said Casey.

'James said it was just a silly game, and he was right,' said Beans.

'Game?' said Casey. 'No way!' And he pulled a piece of black card from his pocket.

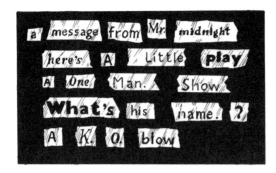

'What's this?' asked Beans, grabbing the card. 'Is it a code message?'

'Don't let anyone else have a look, will you?' grumbled James.

'It's a message from "Mr Midnight",' said Casey.

'We can see that, but who is Mr Midnight?'

'Someone who has been going round busting up the sideshows in Wonderland. But *before* he busts them up, he leaves little messages saying where he's going to strike next. They're a kind of early warning system. The cards are clues to places in Wonderland . . . places Mr Midnight intends to wreck.'

'Sounds absolutely stupid to me,' said James.

'According to Mr Denny, who owns Wonderland, Mr Midnight has done a lot of damage and he's frightened there may be more to come. Denny wanted police protection, twenty-four hour surveillance. My dad told him he couldn't spare half his police force to patrol a funfair on the look out for a nutcase vandal. Denny got mad, and stormed out, chucking Mr Midnight's message cards at somebody who just happened to be waiting in the corridor outside . . .'

'You?'

'Me.'

'Where does the Mystery Squad come in?'

'There are two possibilities,' said Casey. 'One is that this is an insurance fraud, with somebody going round breaking up Wonderland in order to claim money from an insurance company for damaged property and loss of business. We could check that out.'

'And the other possibility?' said James.

'Perhaps there is a Mr Midnight, a nutcase, going around wrecking sideshows.'

'MR MIDNIGHT PROWLS PLEASURE PARK!' I said.

Casey looked at me. I think it was the first time he'd really noticed me, he'd been so busy talking.

'What's the matter with you?' he said.

'Eh?'

'Your face is all funny. And your hair. What've you got that old jersey on for? And those glasses?'

Beans started to giggle.

'Shut up, Beans,' I said, and I explained about my Reversashirt.

'It's not a very good disguise,' said Casey. 'I knew it was you.'

'You knew it was me *because* you know me,' I said. 'The disguise isn't meant for people who *know* me. Suppose I was trailing someone who didn't know me? They suspect they're being followed by someone in a jersey and glasses with a bulgy face and wild hair. Then I change my identity. Brilliant!'

'It was my idea,' said James. 'I don't think it would fool anyone for long . . . but even a short time might be helpful, mightn't it?'

'Could be,' said Casey, sounding as if he didn't think much of it.

I blew a bubble at him.

Casey ignored it.

'About Mr Midnight,' he said. 'Who votes for a Mystery Squad investigation?'

My hand shot up.

'Bodge is one,' said Casey.

'Or two, if you reverse him!' said Beans.

I held her hand up, for revenge.

'Leggo,' said Beans.

'Are you voting or aren't you?' asked Casey.

'All right,' said Beans.

'Beans makes two, and I'm three. How about you James? Are you in favour of the Mystery Squad tackling Mr Midnight?'

'Okay,' said James. 'So long as we don't run into any more trouble with your dad.'

Even Mystery Squad investigations go wrong sometimes. We thought we'd caught a burglar at the baths. He turned out to be the chairman of Casey's dad's police committee. The burglar wasn't very pleased, and neither was Casey's dad!

'What does your dad say about us tackling Mr Midnight, Casey?' Beans asked. It was Beans who'd taken the burglar's clothes, after we'd locked him in the shower cubicle.

'My dad doesn't know we're going to!' said Casey. 'Anyway, he hasn't got enough men to keep an eye on Wonderland all the time and policemen tend to get noticed at a funfair. We won't. We'll just walk around, mingle with the crowd and see if we can spot anything.'

'Wait a bit,' said Beans. 'We ought to investigate

the scene of the crime first. Mr Midnight has already been at work, hasn't he? He's been busting up some of the sideshows and leaving his calling cards. Like this one. Why don't we go and take a look?'

'She's right,' said James. 'We ought to begin at the scene of the crime.'

'If we knew where it was!' said Casey.

'In Wonderland,' I said.

'Yes, but *where* in Wonderland?'

'We'll have to walk round till we see something that's been wrecked,' said James. 'Shouldn't take long.'

'I'll take the dodgems,' I said quickly.

'Don't be silly,' said Beans. 'This card left by Mr Midnight tells us exactly where to look.'

Where would you look?

Roller Disco? Turn to **2**.

Dodgems? Turn to **13**.

Tanner's Traditional Punch and Judy? Turn to **18**.

The House of Wax? Turn to **44**.

Robert Witching's Magic Museum? Turn to **108**.

Ken's Krazy Kastle? Turn to **73**.

Zandra's Wild Animals? Turn to **97**.

Ski-Rider? Turn to **83**.

Mini Grand Prix? Turn to **124**.

Top Score Darts? Turn to **19**.

Water Shute? Turn to **33**.

Loden's Paddle Boats? Turn to **28**.

Dark's Wall of Death? Turn to **65**.

Ridep's Hall of Mirrors? Turn to **113**.

Skinner's Ghost Train? Turn to **57**.

92

Turn to **49**.

93

You've gone wrong. Turn to **30** and try again.

94

Wrong. Turn to **16**.

95

Wrong. Turn to **112** and try again.

Detective Rating

2 points if you got it straight away.
1 point if you needed help.

96

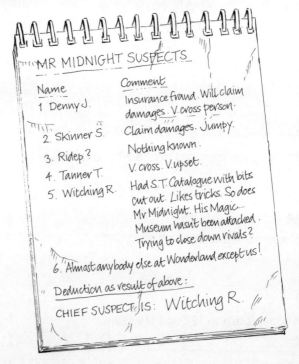

'The "Smart Tricks" catalogue was in Robert Witching's desk,' said James.

   'Oh,' said Beans. 'Great! But . . .'

   'But what?'

'Well, surely we should have told Casey's dad, even if he was yelling at us. I mean, the catalogue is absolute, conclusive proof . . . isn't it?'

'No,' Casey shook his head.

'Witching could have denied it was his,' said James.

'Maybe it *isn't* his. It could have been *planted* on him,' said Casey.

'I bet it wasn't,' said Beans.

'Proving it is another thing,' said Casey.

'Anyway, Robert Witching is confirmed as our Chief Suspect,' I said, and I put it down in my TSM book.

'That's *funny*,' said Beans, looking at my list.

'What is?'

'Funny I didn't spot it before, I mean. My sort of clue.'

'Eh?'

'Well . . . you know Mr Midnight likes leaving his signature on things . . . like using "twelve" in the countdown signs?'

'Yes.'

'I think I know why he chose the name Mr Midnight in the first place,' said Beans. 'In fact *if* Robert Witching *is* Mr Midnight he chose his name very carefully!'

'What?'

'It's another one of his jokes!' said Beans.

WITCHING R. = Mr Midnight

'Midnight,' said Beans, 'is known as the witching hour. Get it? Witching, R?'

'Oh no!' groaned Casey.

'We've got to keep close to Robert Witching, and see if we can catch him in the act,' said James.

'Easier said than done,' said Beans. 'Witching has made enough trouble for us already, and he knows *exactly* what we look like. He isn't going to like being trailed around Wonderland by the Mystery Squad.'

'Bodger?' said James.

'What?' I said.

'Your *Reversashirt*!' said James.

'One Reversashirted Bodger!' said James. 'Witching will never recognise him!'

'Still looks like an ape to me,' said Beans.

'Shut up Beans!' said Casey.

I took no notice of her because I was about to go into action as a Mystery Squad Double Identity Agent!

'You tail Witching, but you don't try anything clever, Bodge,' said Casey, nervously.

I nodded.

'No dramatics!' James warned.

'We'll be close behind you,' said Casey. 'Don't worry if he spots you . . . he probably won't take much notice, because he won't recognise you. He'll think you're just some kid playing about.'

'Makes you look really different,' said Beans. 'Human, almost.'

'We could be in trouble if he spots us, and recognises us,' said James. 'So we'll keep out of the way. You tail him, and we'll tail you . . . at a distance.'

'Okay,' I said.

'You're sure you can do it, Bodge?' said Beans. 'Maybe . . . maybe I should go instead?'

'It's my Double Identity kit!' I said, fiercely. She wasn't going to do me out of the exciting bit.

'Your ugly mug would be recognised right away, Beans,' said Casey, and Beans didn't even say her mug wasn't ugly.

We didn't get talking about it any more, because at that moment we were interrupted. An alarm bell started ringing.

'What's that?' Casey said.

Then we saw what it was. It was too easy to see. Clouds of smoke were coming from the House of Wax.

'He's done it again!' said Casey, bitterly.

We ran towards the House of Wax. The frail walls were well alight, and smoke was belching through the gaps in the canvas roof.

'Somebody's trapped . . . there, at the window!' Beans shouted.

'Going to rescue him, are you?' said Casey.

'No but . . .'

'What's burning, Beans?' said James.

'The House of Wax.'

'What's in the House of Wax?'

'Models of old kings and things,' said Beans. 'But . . .'

'Do you want to bail out of a burning building

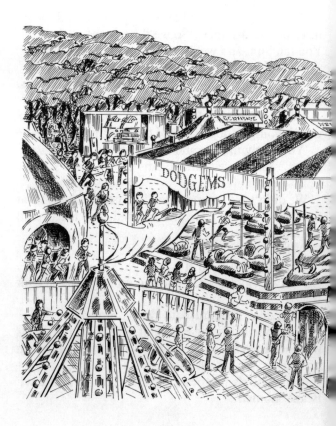

clutching a wax model of Dracula?' asked James, grinning.

'Oh,' said Beans.

'Feeling stupid?' said James.

I would have joined in, but I had spotted something much more important than a burning wax model . . .

What did I spot?

The fire spreading to the next sideshow? Turn to **35**.

Robert Witching leaving the scene? Turn to **8**.

A real person trapped in the House of Wax? Turn to **85**.

Mr Denny leaving the scene? Turn to **79**.

97
Turn to **91** and try again.

98
Wrong. Turn to **42**.

99
Wrong. Go to **81** and try again.

100
Wrong. Turn to **31**.

101
Wrong. Try again. Turn to **10**.

102
Wrong. Turn to **112** and try again.

103
Wrong. Turn to **16**.

104
Turn to **18** and try again.

Detective Rating

3 points if you got it straight away.
1 point if you needed a clue.

105

'What clear evidence?' I asked. Beans was standing looking as if she knew, but she didn't.

'The map,' said Casey. 'There was a map of Wonderland in Dad's briefcase.'

'That doesn't mean he's investigating this case, does it?' I objected.

'Doesn't it?' said Casey. 'I know Dad. He's not investigating the drains.'

'So what do we do now?' asked James.

'Inspect the evidence,' said Beans.

'Yes. The notes from Mr Midnight. But we haven't got them any more.'

'Haven't we?' said Casey.

One of Mr Midnight's cards was lying on the crate we were using as a table.

Who took the card?

James? Turn to **78**.
Beans? Turn to **47**.
Bodger? Turn to **87**.
Casey? Turn to **122**.
Somebody else? Turn to **61**.

106
Wrong. Turn to **42**.

107
Turn to **18** and try again.

108
Turn to **91** and try again.

109
Wrong! Turn to **49**.

110
Wrong! Turn to **43**.

111
Now where?

Detective Rating

2 points if you got it right.
1 point if you needed a clue.

112

'Ridep's Hall of Mirrors,' said Beans. 'Ridep is an anagram of Pride. An image is what you see in a mirror, and if it is cracked from side to side that means that somebody has been smashing up Ridep's Hall of Mirrors.'

Beans is pretty clever sometimes (ugly clever I mean).

We set off to find the Hall of Mirrors.

'What are we looking for?' Beans asked, as we came to a stop outside it.

'We'll start by looking for James's countdown signs,' said Casey. 'Each one so far has had Mr Midnight's jokey signature "twelve" and another number. Toby Tanner's was five and Skinner's was four so this one ought to be three. We're looking for three/twelve.'

'Or six/twelve,' said James. 'We don't know what order the cards came in, do we? This might have been the first job he pulled.'

'If there is such a thing as a countdown sign,' said Casey, doubtfully. 'Maybe the other two were just coincidences.'

'I don't think I believe in coincidences,' said James.

'They happen,' said Casey.

We went inside. We didn't have to pay, because there was nobody at the cash desk. There was nobody at the cash desk, because there were no mirrors in the Hall of Mirrors . . . or almost none.

We started looking for clues.

'There must be a clue somewhere,' Beans said, in a puzzled voice.

What did we find?

A clue on the mirror? Turn to **36**.
A clue on the floor? Turn to **121**.
A clue on the boxes? Turn to **54**.
A clue on the brush shaft? Turn to **95**.
Some other clue? Turn to **102**.
Nothing? Turn to **25**.

113

Turn to **91** and try again.

114

Wrong. Turn to **42**.

115

Turn to **18** and try again.

116

Did she let it go to her head? Turn to **81**.

117

Wrong. Turn to **49**.

118

You are struck by a Cardust Sipe.
Turn to **112**.

119

Right. How can you disprove the story using the positions of Robert Witching, the fire engine and the ice cream van?

On to 68.

120

Turn to 18 and try again.

121

Wrong. Turn to 112 and try again.

122

Wrong. Turn to 105.

123

Wrong. Turn to 42.

124

Turn to 91 and try again.

125

Turn to 81.

The Mystery Squad Detective Rating

This chart will show you the Detective Rating you've earned by completing this Solve it Yourself Mystery.

You should be able to improve your score as you tackle further mysteries in the series and pick up more tips from them. Keep a note of your scores for future reference.

Your Score	Detective Rating
60-70	Sherlock Holmes!
50-59	Super Sleuth!
40-49	Ace Detective
30-39	Detective—1st Class
20-29	Detective—2nd Class
11-19	Junior Detective
6-10	Trainee
0-5	Beginner

If you've enjoyed reading this Solve it Yourself Mystery and would like to test your detective skills further, here are some more titles in the same series:

The Mystery Squad and the Dead Man's Message
The Mystery Squad and the Artful Dodger
The Mystery Squad and the Whistling Teeth